Little
GOLDEN BEAR

K. L. Ning

illustrated by Doina cociuba terrano

Book Publishers Network
P. O. Box 2256
Bothell, WA 98041
425-483-3040
www.bookpublishersnetwork.com

Copyright © 2014 K. L. Ning
Illustrations by Doina Cociuba Terrano

10 9 8 7 6 5 4 3 2 1

ISBN   978-1-940598-35-2
LCCN   2014938655

For Eric and Sam

the Black Bear Family

The black bear family lives in the mountains of the Olympic National Park. They live in the forest among the tall cedar, fir, and pine trees. They are Daddy Bear, Mommy Bear, Little Golden Bear, and his brothers and sisters.

Little Golden Bear is called "little" because he is the smallest among his brothers and sisters. He is called "golden" because he has a golden coat. Also, his paws are pink. Little golden bear is different from his brothers and sisters. His brothers and sisters all have black fur and brown paws.

In the Olympic National Park, there are snow-capped peaks, clear and cool streams, and dark forests full of animals, birds, and trees.

In the spring, the warm sun melts the snow on the mountain tops, and the melting snow trickles down to the streams and into the rivers.

In the summer and in the fall, wild flowers and berries cover the meadows with color. Trees and shrubs are laden with fruits and nuts for the animals and birds to eat.

In the winter, the bear family hibernates. They take a long, long nap.

Little Golden Bear Goes Fishing

The black bear family is just waking up from their long winter's nap. Little Golden Bear is still asleep.

Mommy Bear wakes up Little Golden Bear. She says to Little Golden Bear, "Wake up, my dear. We need to find food."

Little Golden Bear yawns and stands up.

Mommy Bear leads her children to the river bank to look for fish. She knows this is a good spot to catch fish. She sees a lot of silvery salmon jumping up in the water and struggling to go upstream to their spawning ground.

Mommy Bear says to her children. "You all need to learn how to catch a fish. Let me show you."

She wades into the river, and the water comes up to her knees. She catches one of the salmon jumping out of the water.

She says to her children, "See! That's what you do to catch a fish."

Little Golden Bear's brothers and sisters bravely wade into the water from the river bank. Soon, they learn to do what Mommy Bear showed them, and they can catch fish.

Now, it is Little Golden Bear's turn. He stands at the edge of the water, trying to put one foot in slowly and carefully. He quickly pulls his foot out of the water and says, "The water is too cold!"

Mommy Bear says, "Little Golden Bear, try again."

Little Golden Bear puts his feet into the water very, very slowly. He tries to walk toward his mother.

The sand and rocks on the bottom of the river are moving with the rapidly flowing water. Little Golden Bear turns around quickly and runs back to the river bank again. He yells to his mommy, "The water is not too cold. But, the river bottom is moving, and I am afraid I will sink and fall into the water."

Mommy Bear calls out to Little Golden Bear, "Try again, my dear. You will know how to swim if you fall into the water."

Little Golden Bear now puts his feet into the water and very bravely takes a few steps. He does not fall. He is wading into the middle of the river just like his mommy.

He sees the silvery salmon jumping all around him. He scoops up one big fish just like his mommy. Now, Little Golden Bear has learned how to fish for himself.

The black bear family is very happy today for all the fish they have caught.

Mommy Bear is happy because Little Golden Bear has learned how to catch a fish, even if he is afraid to step into the clear, cool, and rapidly flowing water.

Little Golden Bear Goes Hunting

Daddy Bear says to his children, "Let's go to the meadow to find some food to eat."

Daddy Bear walks with his children out of the forest to the big meadow on the mountainside, where it is covered with colorful wild flowers and all kinds of berries. There are blueberries, blackberries, and orange-colored salmonberries.

Daddy Bear also likes to look for honey. Honey is his favorite food.

Little Golden Bear is different from his
brothers and sisters not only because he is
little and golden but also for other reasons.
He does not run as fast as his brothers and
sisters. He does not climb as high as his
brothers and sisters.

But, unlike his brothers and sisters,
Little Golden Bear can smell honey from far,
far away.

On the meadow, Little Golden Bear is always the first to find a hollow log with a bees' nest in it because he can smell honey from far, far away.

The bees' nest is called a beehive. The bees guard their hive carefully. They swarm and sting whoever disturbs their hive.

But, the bears have thick fur coats to protect themselves from bee stings. They have no problem getting the honey from the beehive.

Little Golden Bear calls out to his daddy and his brothers and sisters. "I have found a log with bees and honey!"

Little Golden Bear is always eager to share what he finds. He does not eat the honey all by himself.

After the bear family has eaten all the berries they want, they follow Little Golden Bear to the log full of honey.

The black bear family has a very good day of hunting.

Daddy Bear says to his children, "I am very proud of Little Golden Bear. He is different. He does not run very fast. He does not climb very high. But, he can always find honey, and he shares."

All the bears are very happy with their bellies full of berries and honey. Now, they are going back to the forest to have a rest.

Little Golden Bear Meets Humans

People come to the Olympic National Park to camp, to fish, and to hike. They set up tents in the forest. They bring food with them, and they cook over campfires.

They hike the trails. They watch the animals and birds. They also hope to see bears.

Little Golden Bear and his brothers and sisters like to play in the forest. They climb trees. They roll on the leafy forest floor. They chase squirrels.

Little Golden Bear does not run as fast as his brothers and sisters. Little Golden Bear does not climb as high as his brothers and sisters.

But, he is always curious about everything in the forest.

One day, while playing in the forest, they come close to a campground and see humans. They smell the food cooking over the campfire from a distance. Little Golden Bear and his brothers and sisters all say together, "It smells good. Let's go see what is over there."

23

Little Golden Bear and his brothers and sisters go into the campground.

Suddenly, the humans spot the bears. They try to hide and drop themselves onto the ground. The humans are not moving at all.

The bears think there cannot be any danger from these humans and go closer to the campfire.

Just as the bears are picking up the food, a loud BOOM is heard in the forest. A man on the other side of the campground fired a gun into the air trying to scare the bears away. It works. Startled by the noise, the bears drop the food onto the ground, but they still want to eat it.

Little Golden Bear is curious about the noise and the man. He stands up very, very tall to have a better look at the man with a gun. Then he walks very bravely closer to the man to see what was making the noise.

Daddy Bear and Mommy Bear also heard the noise from the gunshot. They hurry to the campground to look for their children.

The man with the gun sees a golden bear coming toward him. There are many bears following behind the golden bear. He becomes alarmed and afraid. He turns around quickly, runs as fast as he can, and disappears into the forest on the other side of the woods.

Daddy Bear and Mommy Bear are glad that Little Golden Bear was brave enough to walk toward the man and make him run away.

They tell their children to leave the other humans alone.

Soon, they are all back in the forest and away from danger.

Acknowledgements

On a rainy day, what else is better to do than make up stories with grandchildren? I have my grandkids to thank for the idea of a bear story. Special thanks are due for Jane B. Goepper, Michael N. Wong, and Marian McLeod for suggestions in writing down the stories. Claire Hensler and Julie Scandora pointed me in the right direction to have the stories put into a book. Sheryn Hara introduced me to Doina Cociuba Terrano, who is not only a versatile and wonderful artist but also a great teacher and a true friend. I appreciated all the help given me to have the stories appear in printed form.